Pirate Pete's
Potty
STICKER BOOK

**Pirate Pete is a little boy.
Can you help him learn to use the potty?
Find the stickers in the middle of the book
and put them in the correct places.**

Hello, Pirate Pete!

Pirate Pete wears a nappy underneath his trousers.
He uses nappies to do wees and poos in.

Give Pete a big,
piratey hat.

Well done!
Add a star!

Nappies or pants?

Pirate Pete wants to wear pants like his mummy, daddy and big sister.

Daddy pants   **Nappies**   **Big girl pants**   **Mummy pants**

Pieces of Eight

8

Stick in Pete and his mummy
outside the pirate shop.

Choosing a potty

At the shop, Pirate Pete and his mummy look for a potty. There are lots to choose from.

Stick Pirate
Pete's favourite
potty here.

What is a potty used for?

Pirate Pete is excited about his new potty. At first he can't remember what to do with it.

Is it a funny hat?

A toy boat?

A very useful storage box?

Stick Pete using the potty the right way here.

Well done!
Add a star!

Sitting on the potty

Pirate Pete's mummy and daddy explain that a potty is for doing wees and poos in. Pete gives it a try.

Find the big sticker of Pete sitting on his potty.

Well done!

Add a star!

Lots of pirate pants!

It's time for Pete to choose some grown-up pirate pants.
They come in all sorts of patterns and colours.

Stick Pirate Pete's
favourite pants here.

Pants up! Pants down!

Pirate Pete likes wearing his special big boy pants.
They make him feel very grown-up.

Pants up!

Pants down!

Put the sticker of Pete with his
pants down here.

Ready to go!

The next time Pete feels like he needs to do a wee or a poo, he sits on his potty.

He waits

and waits

and waits...

until something brilliant happens!

Stick a teeny, tiny little wee into Pete's potty!

Well done!
Add a star!

The pirate potty rules

Pirate Pete's mummy teaches him three
special pirate potty rules.

1. After you have used your potty, ask Mummy or
Daddy to help you wipe your bottom with toilet
paper. Always wipe from front to back.

Stick in Pete helping Mummy.

2. Flush everything away in the toilet.
Don't worry if it makes a loud noise.

Find the sticker
of Pete washing
his hands.

3. Always wash and dry
your hands afterwards.

Well done!
Add a star!

Accidents happen

Sometimes, however, Pirate Pete can't get to the potty in time and makes a mess on the floor.

Stick in Pete's little accident.

Pete's mummy and daddy don't mind.
They still think he is very clever!

Pooing in the potty

Doing a poo in the potty is harder than doing a wee.
Pete keeps on trying. One day, he manages it!

Stick a poo into
Pete's potty.

Well done!
Add a star!

Three cheers for Pete!

Pete shows the full potty to his mummy and daddy.
He shows it to his big sister, and even to the baby.

Everybody CHEERS!

Stick in a picture of Pete's big sister
and baby brother.

A new potty adventure

Now, only Pirate Pete's baby brother wears nappies.
One day, Pete will show him how to use the potty, too.

Stick in Pete and give his
special potty to the baby.

Well done!
Add a star!

My pirate potty reward chart

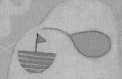

	M	T	W	T	F	S	S
I put on big boy pants							
I sat on the potty							
I asked to use the potty							
I did a wee on the potty							
I did a poo on the potty							
I wiped my bottom							
I washed my hands							
I stayed dry all day